MY MOTHER IS WEIRD

story by
Rachna Gilmore

illustrations by
Brenda Jones

RAGWEED
THE ISLAND PUBLISHER

Text © 1988 by Rachna Gilmore
Illustrations © 1988 by Brenda Jones
ISBN 0-920304-94-X (cloth)
ISBN 0-920304-83-4 (paper)
10   9   8   7   6
Sixth Printing, 1994

*With thanks to The Canada Council and
the Prince Edward Island Council of the Arts for their kind support.*

Book Design by Brenda Jones and Laurie Brinklow
Typesetting by Braemar Publishing Limited
Printed by Wing King Tong Co., Ltd., Hong Kong

Ragweed Press
P.O. Box 2023
Charlottetown, Prince Edward Island
Canada   C1A 7N7

Distributed by
General Distribution Services
30 Lesmil Road
Don Mills, Ontario
Canada M3B 2T6

CANADIAN CATALOGUING IN PUBLICATION DATA

Gilmore, Rachna, 1953–

My mother is weird

ISBN 0-920304-94-X (bound)
ISBN 0-920304-83-4 (pbk.)

I. Jones, Brenda, 1953–. II. Title.

PS8563.I45M9 1988   jC813'.54   C88-098634-4
PZ7.G54My 1988

For Karen Jane

My mother is so weird.

Some mornings when she wakes up, she has horns on her head and long, pointy teeth and claws. She speaks in a voice like a jackhammer.

But after her morning coffee, Mom's horns disappear, and her teeth and claws shrink back to normal. She speaks in a soft, smooth voice.

One morning, the toilet plugged up, the lid fell off my toy box and we ran out of coffee. My mother snapped and growled. The horns grew bigger and bigger. Her eyes were red and her teeth and claws enormous.

When the horns weren't gone by mid-morning, I yelled, "I'm leaving!"

But I yelled quietly, when my mother was using the blender.

I packed my backpack and as soon as my mother went into the bathroom, I shouted, "I'm going to Maria's house!"

"All right!" my mother grunted.

So I left.

Maria's mother is always nice. She never yells. She speaks in a honey voice and she smells pretty.

I rang Maria's doorbell. Maria opened the door.

"Hi," I said. "Can I play with you?"

"Sure," said Maria. "Come on in."

She looked quickly over her shoulder. "But we have to be quiet."

This is weird, I thought. Maria's mother never minds having anyone over. She never minds how much noise we make.

Just then Maria's mother came out of the kitchen. I stared. Maria's mother had horns and claws and pointy teeth. She also had hair growing out of her ears.

"What's going on?" I whispered.

Maria said, "She gets like this sometimes. My baby brother was up six times last night. But don't worry, she's not too bad if we stay out of her way."

We stayed out of her way.

At lunchtime Maria said, "Please stay for lunch."

So I stayed. I didn't eat a lot. When we finished, I said very politely, "Thank you for the lovely lunch."

Maria's mother said, "You're welcome."

But the horns were still there and the claws and pointy teeth and the hair growing out of her ears.

I put on my backpack and said good-bye to Maria.
I ran across the back yard, into my house.

My mother was banging and rattling tools as she fixed my toy box. The horns were still there.

I ran up to her and gave her a big hug.
"I love you," I said.

Then a strange thing happened. The horns disappeared, and the claws and teeth shrank back to normal. And all without coffee!

"I love you, too," said Mom, hugging me.

I know sometimes my mother is weird, but most of the time she isn't.

(But at least she never has hair growing out of her ears.)